WENDY QUILL

is A CROCODILE'S BOTTOM

written by
Wendy Meddour

with drawings by
MINA MAY
(Age 11)

OXFORD
UNIVERSITY PRESS

OXFORD
UNIVERSITY PRESS

Great Clarendon Street, Oxford OX2 6DP
Oxford University Press is a department of the University of Oxford.
It furthers the University's objective of excellence in research, scholarship,
and education by publishing worldwide in

Oxford   New York

Auckland Cape Town Dar es Salaam Hong Kong Karachi
Kuala Lumpur Madrid Melbourne Mexico City Nairobi
New Delhi Shanghai Taipei Toronto

With offices in

Argentina Austria Brazil Chile Czech Republic France Greece
Guatemala Hungary Italy Japan Poland Portugal Singapore
South Korea Switzerland Thailand Turkey Ukraine Vietnam

Oxford is a registered trade mark of Oxford University Press
in the UK and in certain other countries

Text © Wendy Meddour 2013
Illustrations © Mina May 2013

The moral rights of the author have been asserted

Database right Oxford University Press (maker)

First published 2013

British Library Cataloguing in Publication Data

Data available

ISBN: 978-0-19-279463-5

1 3 5 7 9 10 8 6 4 2

Printed in Great Britain
Paper used in the production of this book is a natural,
recyclable product made from wood grown in sustainable forests
The manufacturing process conforms to the environmental
regulations of the country of origin

DEDICATION   **DISCLAIMER**

If any of the characters in this book (especially my wonderful, inspirational parents) bear any resemblance to themselves in real life, please remember that you are completely fictional and this is just a totally surprising coincidence.

Signed: *Wendy Meddour*
(writer)

I'd like to dedicate my drawings to all of my friends. And to my three younger brothers (as long as they promise never to steal any of my lip balms again).

Signed: **Mina May**
(illustrator)

ADDITIONAL INFORMATION:
The above-signed would also like to say a HUGE thank you to Jasmine Richards (brilliant editor), Karen Stewart (brilliant designer), and Penny Holroyde (brilliant agent)—who loved Wendy Quill as much as they did and helped them bring her to life!

CONTENTS

ACT 1 ✱ 3
WENDY QUILL IS A CROCODILE'S BOTTOM

✱ 43 ACT 2
WENDY QUILL'S AMAZING SENSIBLE SHOES

ACT 3 ✱ 115
WENDY QUILL CATCHES THE PLAGUE

ACT 1
WENDY QUILL
is a
CROCODILE'S
BOTTOM

A Wheezy bird in her natural habitat

Everyone calls me *'Wheezy Bird'* because of the way I laugh—a sort of *'giggle, wheeze, giggle, wheeze'*. I can't really help it—it's just the noise that comes out when things are funny. Woody thinks I sound like a sea-lion but that's not true because sea-lions don't actually laugh.

Oh yes we do!

Dad says I'm the only *wheezy bird* in the whole of the British Isles. (He's a birdwatcher and to him, rare birds are way more exciting than nine-year-old girls with freckles and mousey-brown hair.) So I don't really mind being a *wheezy bird* and it could actually be a lot worse. The lollipop lady calls Helen Butterworth 'Little Miss Wet Pants', even though she stopped doing that ages ago.

Wheezy birds are actually quite rare

But then something happened at my school that made me wish people called me my real name—which is actually

WENDY QUILL.

Then Miss Pinch *wouldn't* have forgotten

who I was and I'd probably be

QUITE FAMOUS BY NOW!

Miss Pinch *should* know my name because

she says it every morning at register. I think

she's got 'anaemia' or something—which

is actually quite sad, because it's not nice

when you can't remember things.

A REALLY IMPORTANT FACT:

My big sister Tawny says that 'anaemia' is when your blood isn't working properly—and 'amnesia' is when you forget things. But they sound just the same so I think Miss Pinch probably has both.

Anyway, we'd just finished learning about Romans lying down on cushions and being sick a lot when they ate their food, when Miss Pinch said:

'Children, I have an **exciting announcement** to make.' (Miss Pinch always has 'exciting announcements' to make.) 'This morning, I will be giving out parts for our new school play. Please line up. And remember to form an orderly queue.'

Everyone started pushing to the front, but Tyler Ainsworth grabbed my arm:

My teacher, Miss Pinch, nearly smiling

6

'Hey, *Wheezy Bird*,' he said.
'If it's *Cinderella, you'll* have to be the ugly
sister.' Miss Pinch says I have 'a talent for
answering back', which I do, because I
said: 'There are actually *two* ugly sisters in
Cinderella, Tyler Ainsworth.'

Then I stared at him very hard. But
he didn't notice that I meant *he* should be
an ugly sister, so I blew a raspberry at him

I didn't
blow this
sort of
raspberry

This is Tyler
Ainsworth—
who is sort
of like a bully

Some of these germs are quite cute

instead. (I won't actually do that again because it's 'a hygiene issue' and 'could spread germs'.)

'What's the play, Miss?' asked Sophia Nowitsky. (Sophia Nowitsky always asks important questions because she is 'gifted and talented'.)

Sophia Nowitsky even looks gifted and talented

. . . so do her plaits

'Oh, silly me,' sighed Miss Pinch. 'I'd forget my head, if it wasn't screwed on.'

(This can actually happen to people with ~~anaemia~~ amnesia). 'The play is called

Peter Pan & Wendy.

Some of you might have read the book.'

I hadn't actually just *read* the book.
I *was* the book. Mum called me 'Wendy'
because she loves *Peter Pan* almost
as much as Dad loves birds. (She likes *Heidi*
too and I was called Heidi until I was three
days old but Mum couldn't stop thinking
about goats.) Anyway, Dad let Mum have

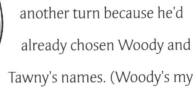

another turn because he'd already chosen Woody and Tawny's names. (Woody's my

My big brother Woody

big brother and he's named after a lesser-spotted-woodpecker and Tawny's my big sister, and she's a type of owl with fluffy wings.)

My big sister Tawny

When Miss Pinch made her **'exciting announcement'**, I felt this huge lump in my tummy. I think it was butterflies but it might have been porridge. Whatever it was, I couldn't believe I was going to be a famous actress! I'd always thought I was going to be a vet. But being 'Wendy'

10

in *Peter Pan* was actually lots better. I'd be able to fight with Captain Hook, bicker with Tinkerbell, and save the lost boys in front of everyone. This was my

ONE BIG CHANCE.

Because Tyler Ainsworth had been so annoying, I was stuck at the back of the queue. I didn't really mind though because grown-ups save the best till last. (Even Tawny does that with orange Smarties and she's just a teenager.) Sophia Nowitsky was at the back too because 'rushing is bad

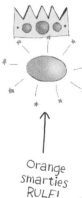

Orange smarties RULE!

for the digestion', so I tapped her on the shoulder and said:

'Miss Pinch will probably make you Tinkerbell because you'd be a *really* good fairy.'

Then I winked at her *and* smiled. I'm *always* nice to Sophia Nowitsky because Mum says you should be nice to people who are different. ('Gifted and talented' people are very different at my school.) Sophia sort of sniffed at me and fiddled with her hair bobble which is another thing that 'gifted and talented' people do. Then Miss Pinch told my best-friend—Florence Hubert—that she was going to be a dog!

A 'gifted and talented' hair bobble

I thought she would be sad but Florence
Hubert has a new golden Labrador called
Prince so she was actually very happy.

Florence Hubert . . .
dreaming of being a dog

'Ah, Sophia,' smiled Miss Pinch,
walking around Sophia like she was

FOR SALE

'Yes. I think that *you* will make the perfect Wendy.'

'Thank you, Miss Pinch.' Sophia beamed and flicked her hair like a real actress.

'But Miss Pinch!' I slightly shouted. **'She *can't* be *Wendy*.'**

'Why ever not?' asked Miss Pinch. She looked annoyed and sort of like a weasel.

'Because,' I explained, '*I actually already am.*'

Miss Pinch peered over her glasses. Her eyes looked like those misty marbles in the bottom of the bag—the ones that nobody wants.

14

'No,' said Miss Pinch, 'you're . . .'

I pulled the best 'Wendy' face that I could. But she just coughed and looked down her list:

'You're . . . the **CROCODILE**.'

Everyone laughed—*even* Florence Hubert (who is *supposed* to be my best friend) *and* her twin brother, Laurence, who doesn't look the same at all!

'But there *isn't* a **CROCODILE** in *Wendy and Peter Pan*,' I said, even though I knew there slightly was.

'Yes there is,' said Sophia Nowitsky. 'The **CROCODILE** chases Captain Hook and swallows a clock.'

She's going to be ME?!

'Thank you, Sophia,' said Miss Pinch.
'I knew we could rely on you.' Then she
passed me the plastic fireman's helmet
that would go under the **CROCODILE'S** head.
'Try this on,' she said.

I put the yellow helmet on but it
slipped down over my nose.

This is me, completely not fitting

'Oh dear,' said Miss Pinch. 'Your head
isn't big enough.' She gave the helmet to

Henna Hussein, who squeezed it on top of
her sky blue hijab. It made her glasses fall off.

This is Henna
Hussein, fitting
perfectly (apart
from her glasses)

'Excellent,' said Miss Pinch.

Henna Hussein didn't say anything.
She's like that. The not-saying-anything
sort.

I tried again. Our school motto is:

Remain staunch in the face of adversity

—which actually means: 'we must always try again'. (I know that for a fact because Woody told me and he's already nearly eleven.)

'Miss Pinch,' I said, 'Sophia Nowitsky *can't* be Wendy because she's got straight black hair. And I've been a "Wendy" for all of my life so I've actually had lots of experience.'

'No, Wendy Quill,' said Miss Pinch, pretending she hadn't forgotten my name at all. 'My mind is made up. You will have to be the CROCODILE'S BOTTOM.'

Wendy is a Little Princess

I AM a real Wendy because I even have a T-Shirt to prove it

. . . I'm not so keen on the 'princess' bit, though!

Tyler Ainsworth

on the floor and

laughed all over the place.

'Get up, Tyler. Floors are for *feet*, not for fun,' said Miss Pinch—which is another thing that she always says.

Suddenly, I knew what was happening. Grandad had warned me about it at the allotment—I was getting one of

'**LIFE'S HARD LESSONS**':

19

'Now then, Ducky (which is what Grandad calls me), if you get one of "**LIFE'S HARD LESSONS**", you must always look on "THE BRIGHT SIDE OF THINGS".'

I ran over to the window. The playground was covered in rain and the sky was full up of clouds. 'THE BRIGHT SIDE OF THINGS' wasn't anywhere! When I turned round, Miss Pinch was giving out copies of the play to Peter Pan, Wendy, Nana, The Lost Boys, Captain Hook, and

Smee. But she didn't give anything to Henna Hussein or me!

'Miss Pinch,' I asked, trying not to cry because that's what babies do. 'Doesn't the **CROCODILE** get any words?'

'No, of course not,' said Miss Pinch. 'It's *just* a **CROCODILE**'.

Miss Pinch ALWAYS knows BEST (but sometimes BEST hurts people's feelings)

'But Miss Pinch!' I answered back. 'Sebastian Thunder was Baloo last year but he got to sing *and* dance *and* everything. And Baloo is *just* a bear.'

'That was *Jungle Book*,' said Miss Pinch. '*Peter Pan and Wendy* is a totally different story.'

I was trying to think how to answer

back again when Florence Hubert, who is still

my best friend (even though she laughed at

the **CROCODILE** bottom bit), said:

'Miss Pinch. Wendy Quill *should* get

some words because she's the best in

the class at talking.'

I nodded a lot because this was a

SCIENTIFIC FACT.

I am also
very good
at nodding

ACT 1

'Hmmmm,' said Miss Pinch, squeezing her lips together like a cat's bottom (which is a little bit rude but true). 'You do have a point, Florence Hubert. I suppose there's no harm if the **CROCODILE** says:

"Tick Tock",

'Thank you, Miss Pinch!' I said. I felt happy all over but Henna Hussein looked like she was going to be sick (she doesn't like saying words in front of people).

'It's all right, Henna Hussein. I'll do all the "Tick Tocks",' I said, kindly. (Mum says you must always be kind to shy people because it's 'quite an affliction'. I don't know exactly what this is but I'm glad I haven't got it.) I think Henna Hussein was about to

say something back when Tyler Ainsworth

threw a rubber at my head because he's

'hyper' and eats chocolate bars for lunch.

Then Sophia Nowitsky waved her hand in

the air like she really needed the toilet:

'I've got an idea, Miss Pinch,' she said,

all full of excitement.

'Why don't you let Wendy

Quill be my understudy?'

'No, dear. Not this time,' said Miss Pinch.

Which is actually a good thing,

because I don't like studying anyway.

And definitely not *under* Sophia Nowitsky!

Tyler Ainsworth likes
throwing rubbers at
my head

24

ANOTHER IMPORTANT FACT:
Tawny says an 'understudy' is actually the person who gets to say your words on stage when you have a tummy ache or a sore throat. I still don't want to be Sophia Nowitsky's one though. Even if she's poorly.

THWACK!!

Tyler Rules

On the night of the

'GRAND OPENING',

everybody came to watch. Grandad even turned his hearing aid on. I felt a bit scared at first because we had to wait behind the fire exit covered in a scratchy dark green cloth.

My head DOES NOT like Tyler Ainsworth's rubbers being thrown at it! Ouch!

25

The page before . . .
Being a crocodile's bottom is actually really good fun

'Are you all right?' asked Florence Hubert (even though she was a dog).

I peered out from under the tail.

'**Yes**,' I said. 'But when you're a **CROCODILE**, timing is very important and it's easy to get it wrong.'

She wagged her tail and smiled.

That is why she is my best friend.

My best-friend Florence Hubert in her AMAZING fluffy dog costume

Suddenly, Henna Hussein started to cry.

'What's the matter?' I asked, getting

back inside the darkness.

'My new glasses don't fit under the helmet,' she

said in a tiny voice. 'So I can't even see.'

'There's no time for tears,' said Miss

Pinch. 'It's nearly your turn to go on.' She

tapped the **CROCODILE'S** papier-mâché head

rather hard.

ANOTHER IMPORTANT FACT:

Miss Pinch is always getting us to make things
out of papier-mâché in class—especially **CROCODILE**
heads. It's just newspaper and glue, really. But
completely French. And then we have to use
paints from our own country.

'Ouch!' cried Henna Hussein.

'Miss Pinch,' I shouted through the scratchy cloth. 'Shall I go at the front? I think my head's grown and I'm *very* good at seeing things.'

'No,' said Miss Pinch. 'Stay exactly where you are. You're too short and your head is too small.'

'Oh,' I said, because I had lost the argument.

Suddenly, Miss Pinch

 **PUSHED** me

from behind—

even though

I couldn't see her at all.

she said,

SHOVING

us

through

the doors.

31

It was very quiet on the stage.

Completely quiet.

I could only hear my

moonboots squeaking on the floor.

'I don't know where I am,' sniffed Henna Hussein, without her glasses that wouldn't fit.

'It's all right,' I said, kindly. 'Nor do I.'

'We're over here,' whispered Tinkerbell (who was actually Angelina Hardthorpe).

Some of the grown-ups laughed.

'I want to go home,' said Henna Hussein.

'But remember,' I said, 'we're being a

CROCODILE and it's a very important job. Just

go forwards and sort of to the side.'

But we went to the wrong side and

bumped into lots of things.

'Ouch!' said Angelina Hardthorpe.

Here are
both of my
legs getting
a little bit
famous

But it didn't really matter because everyone was clapping (I know because I had a quick peek). Even Grandad was clapping and he's normally doing something else. We didn't actually chase

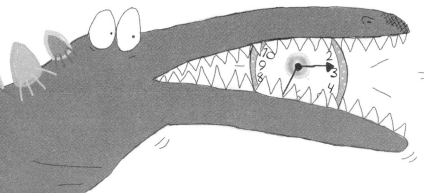

Captain Hook (because that was Laurence Hubert and we couldn't find him), but we *did* remember to swallow the clock completely on time.

Please DO NOT try this at home! Swallowing clocks can be DANGEROUS

36

After we'd done all the important **CROCODILE** bits, Miss Pinch came onto the stage. (She wasn't actually *supposed* to come onto the stage, but teachers don't like standing behind doors because they're used to standing at the front.)

'OH DEAR THE SHOW MUST GO ON!'

she said, pushing us out of the fire exit.

Anyway, the show did go on and we were totally BRILLIANT. Dad told me I said 'Tick Tock' in all the right

places and 'virtually stole the show', and
Mum took lots of pictures and felt 'proud as
punch' (I'm the one at the back in flowery
leggings and brand new moonboots).

Grandad said no one even noticed when
we knocked over the scenery and fell on
top of Tinkerbell. The whole thing was

Photographs are
VERY IMPORTANT
because they help you
NOT to forget

a complete success (and definitely good practice for being a **CROCODILE** in real life). But I can't help thinking that if Miss Pinch didn't have anaemia, and everyone remembered my real name, I'd actually be quite famous by now.

ACT 2
WENDY ♥ QUILL'S
AMAZING
SENSIBLE
SHOES

I think you might completely love this story

Most people in the world have really nice shoes. My big sister has shiny ones with heels that go 'click', Henna Hussein's got pointy ones with buckles on, and Florence Hubert wears purple trainers even though they make her feet sweat. But Mum says that 'feet are for life' and 'the right footwear

My sister's 'clicketty' shoes

Click Click Click

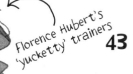
Florence Hubert's 'yucketty' trainers

Henna Hussein's 'buckletty' shoes

43

is essential' at my age. So she buys me

—you know, the ones they hide at the

back of the shop—with 'T-BARS' and

'EXTRA SUPPORT'.

Dad's toes are very, very wonky

Dad says sensible shoes are a 'complete waste of money'. But Mum huffs and points at Dad's toes (which are sort of wonky and all squeezed together).

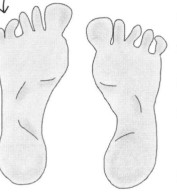

Mum's fingers are very, very pointy

'It's a well-known fact,' says Dad, 'that Quill feet have been like this for generations.'

'Nonsense,' says Mum, 'WRONG SHOES.'

But Dad is actually right though. Sensible shoes *are* 'a complete waste of money' and I have to sit on mine at break

45

time, otherwise Angelina Hardthorpe

whispers about them to her friends.

(Angelina Hardthorpe's friends are not my

friends because you can't be in 'the girly

whisper whisper whis whisper per

Sitting on my shoes and pretending they're not there

whisper whisper whisper whisper

gang' unless you wear pointy shoes and

have your ears pierced.)

Mum says that if you *don't* wear

sensible shoes, you'll end up walking

like 'a bow-legged chicken'. But
Angelina Hardthorpe *doesn't* walk
like a bow-legged chicken. And
bow-legged chickens *don't* wear
pointy shoes. So it can't be a
SCIENTIFIC FACT.

'Just you wait,' says Mum.
'You'll see.'

Angelina
Hardthorpe
walking
normally

But I've been waiting for ages and
Angelina Hardthorpe *still* walks like she's
completely normal.

Anyway, it's not easy sitting on your
shoes all the time and I completely HATED
them until Mum had to work late at the
library. But now I actually **LOVE** them.

47

A bow-legged
chicken—walking
like a bow-legged
chicken

Because if I *hadn't* been wearing my

AMAZING, SENSIBLE SHOES when I went

tap-dancing with the Hubert twins,

 then I'd *never* have been picked for a

It all started when Miss Pinch made

me 'partners' with Tyler Ainsworth.

She told us to 'put our heads together'

(which I didn't because everybody

48

knows that Tyler Ainsworth has nits)

and make a poster 'advertising' an

'Let's do a Hamster Beach-Hut,' I said

to Tyler Ainsworth.

You see, we've got this hamster called

Twitch and all he does is go round and

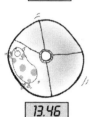

`09.20`

`13.46`

`21.38`

Hamsters are always very busy

But sometimes they need to relax

round in his wheel. It's not his fault—*all* hamsters are like that. But if Twitch had a Hamster Beach-Hut, he would be much more exciting. He could go to the seaside and not get sunburnt or eaten by hungry seagulls.

'That idea is stupider than you,' grunted Tyler Ainsworth.

'*Actually*, Tyler Ainsworth, it's a really good idea,' I said, standing up.

'SIT DOWN, WENDY QUILL,'

said Miss Pinch.

50

ACT 2

I
SAT
DOWN

even though you should always

STAND UP

to bullies.

'Well, Tyler Ainsworth *does* have a point,' said Sophia Nowitsky. 'A Hamster Beach-Hut is a silly idea because hamsters *never* get sunburnt and seagulls just eat chips.'

That's when I found out that 'gifted and talented' people can sometimes actually be wrong!

'I'm sorry, Sophia Nowitsky,' I said, 'but *my* dad is a *real* birdwatcher and he

Sophia Nowitsky getting it completely WRONG!

NO WE DON'T!

says that "*all gulls are scavengers and eat anything left on the beach*". And *everybody* knows that sunburnt hamsters taste way better than greasy old chips.'

Suddenly, Tyler Ainsworth grabbed my arm!

Tyler Ainsworth isn't even Chinese at all!

'If you don't do a poster for CHOCOLATE TOOTHPASTE, I'll give you a Chinese burn,' he sort of growled.

I stood up again and told him that he *couldn't* actually give me a Chinese burn because he *wasn't* actually from China.

'I THOUGHT I TOLD YOU TO SIT DOWN!'

shouted Miss Pinch.

It doesn't seem exactly fair when the headmaster tells you to stand up to bullies, and the teacher tells you to sit down to them.

53

(I don't like it when grown-ups can't make up their minds.) I didn't say anything back though because Miss Pinch was opening an envelope that was actually all about me!

Miss Pinch always knows things about ME before I do

'Wendy Quill,' she said, fiddling with her scratchy necklace, 'after school, you must go home with the Hubert twins. Your mother's working late at the library.'

'But Miss Pinch,' I answered back politely, 'I *can't* go with the Hubert twins—even though Florence Hubert is my best friend. You see, I've got Textile Club tonight and we're making toads out of buttons and socks.'

All about Wendy. All about Wendy. All about Wendy.

54

'Please do as you are told,' said Miss Pinch.

Tyler Ainsworth laughed and started flicking bits out of his nose.

'TYLER AINSWORTH!' shrieked Miss Pinch, 'IS *THAT HOW YOU'D BEHAVE AT HOME*?'

Tyler Ainsworth looked confused because everybody knows he behaves a lot worse at home and even his nan swears in the playground. But I think Miss Pinch had forgotten because she's got lots of anaemia.

I completely LOVE toads made out of buttons and socks

When the bell went, Ms Hubert was waiting in the playground talking to her friends with smart hair. She smiled with all her lipstick and gave both of the twins a chocolate brioche with lots of real chocolate inside. (I didn't really mind though because I wasn't actually very hungry anyway (much).)

'Wendy Quill,' said Ms Hubert, 'I'm afraid that the twins have tap-dancing lessons tonight. You'll just have to sit on the side.'

'Oh. Thank you,' I smiled. 'Sitting on the side is what I do best.'

'I see?!' said Ms Hubert—which is what grown-ups say when they don't.

Before she'd gone to be late at the library,
Mum had dropped some of my best
play clothes at the Hubert's house—so I
put them on as quick as a flash while
Florence Hubert brushed her teeth.
(Ms Hubert is very fussy about teeth.)
Then, we got in the Huberts' car and
drove to the Higglesbottom Art Centre.
I waited in the corridor while Ms Hubert
helped the twins get changed. (They can
do 'normal' clothes on their own but
tights can be *very* tricky.) When they
came out, something awful happened
completely by accident:

58

Giggle wheeze, giggle wheeze, giggle wheeze.

I didn't mean to but I was

giggle-wheezing all over again!

Laurence Hubert's tights had made me do it!

'Stop laughing!' said Florence Hubert.

'Or everyone will call you *Wheezy Bird*

instead of Wendy Quill! Then you'll *never* be

a little bit famous!'

Boys in tights can sometimes look funny

giggle wheeze
giggle wheeze
giggle wheeze

SOME IMPORTANT INFORMATION:

If you don't know about the time I was a **CROCODILE'S** bottom, then that bit won't make sense. But it doesn't really matter because you probably know all about it anyway.

'I...

giggle wheeze ...

can't...

giggle wheeze ...

stop...

giggle wheeze ...

laughing,' I sort of said.

61

'Quick!' said Florence Hubert.
'Do **THE SPECIAL TRICK!**'
THE SPECIAL TRICK is completely
top secret so I can only tell you if you tick a
very important box:

 (tick here please)

Oh! But if this is not actually your book,
you'd better not write in it or you'll get
into REALLY BIG TROUBLE. So you'll
have to do a 'PINKY SWEAR' instead.
Lock your little fingers together and say:

'I promise not to tell anyone about
THE SPECIAL TRICK. Even if they say
they'll give me money or sweets.'

OK . . . now it is all safe:

TOTALLY TOP SECRET INFORMATION:

SPECIAL TRICK 1: HOW TO STOP *GIGGLE WHEEZING*
(Invented by Wendy Quill and Florence Hubert)

1) First, put your hand over your mouth to make the *giggle wheeze* quieter

2) Close all of your eyes

3) The next bit is really important . . .
Try very hard to think about . . .

DEAD CATS

(**POORLY CATS** work too, but it takes longer.)

WARNING:
Never think about
when your cat
got run over unless
you want to cry.

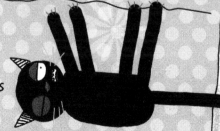

Anyway, I did **THE SPECIAL TRICK** and it worked! The *giggle wheezing* stopped almost straight away. When I opened my eyes, Ms Hubert was still talking:

'There's nothing whatsoever wrong with boys in tights, Wendy Quill.'

'No, there is completely not,' I said, thinking about **DEAD CATS** again.

Florence Hubert winked at me to say 'well done'. But I'd done **THE SPECIAL TRICK** too well!

ME . . . doing the 'SPECIAL TRICK' too well

Florence Hubert ALWAYS makes me smile

That's why she's my bestest ever friend

'Don't cry!' said Florence Hubert. 'You were AMAZING.'

I wiped my nose and smiled. I'm glad that Florence Hubert is my best friend.

'Come along,' said Ms Hubert, pushing Laurence Hubert and his tights down the corridor. 'We don't want to miss the auditions.'

I followed the Hubert twins into a hall that smelt of cheese and grown-up armpits—but it was actually full of leg-warmers and tights.

'Will you watch me?' asked Florence Hubert.

I nodded a 'yes' but I was still too full up of tears to talk out loud. (Next time, I will only think about **SLIGHTLY POORLY CATS**—unless it's a complete emergency.)

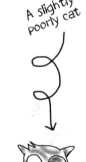

A slightly poorly cat

66

Everyone started doing funny things in front of a huge long mirror. Ms Hubert told me they were '*S-T-R-E-T-C-H-I-N-G*' and that '*S-T-R-E-T-C-H-I-N-G*' is a very important part of exercise.

But no one was doing it right and they all stayed exactly the same size.

Everybody not getting bigger

'Can I go and sit on the side now, please?' I asked Ms Hubert. (I had a big list of things to think about and didn't want to run out of time.)

'Off you go then,' said Ms Hubert.

I got out my special notebook and looked at my '**LIST OF THINGS TO THINK ABOUT WHEN SITTING ON THE SIDE**':

💜 Can butterflies go backwards?

💜 Why do brains smell of cheese?

💜 Why do some monkeys have blue bottoms?

💜 Can you eat with your toes?

💜 Why aren't cows camouflaged?

ACT 2

I was already busy thinking about
Number 2 (which I *know* is a SCIENTIFIC
FACT because I read about it in Woody's
book called *Odd Facts about the Brain*),
when the lady in a tracksuit and a sparkly
top said: 'Would you like to join in?'

'No thank you,' I said. 'I'm busy
thinking. And anyway, I'm not
wearing tights.'

I was actually wearing
my favourite stripy trousers
and my 'Wendy is a Little
Princess' T-shirt. (I don't really like the
'princess' bit but Mum said it was the only
one at the market and 'beggars can't be

Wendy is a Little Princess

Please don't look
at the 'little
princess' bit

choosers'—which is not like Mum because she normally pays for things.)

'Oh,' laughed the lady in the sparkly top, 'clothes aren't important—so long as you've got your shoes. Come on, join in behind Florence Hubert.'

Clothes are actually *very* important and I'd feel completely silly without them. But everyone was looking at me so I put my list away and did as I was told.

'Miss Shuffle thinks you're wearing tap shoes!' giggled Florence Hubert. 'But they haven't got any tap,' I giggled back.

Ha Ha Ha Ha

The lady in the important top is actually called Miss Shuffle

70

Just then, a man with a tight white vest and a tummy danced into the room. He looked happy and his hair bounced— even though he wore a squashy headband.

'My dears,' he said, 'it's time to begin the auditions. Just wait for the intro and

The man with the tummy is actually called Clive

follow me.' He spread his arms out and looked at the ceiling. Then the piano started to play.

The piano lady has beautifully tinkly fingers

Suddenly, Florence Hubert started clopping her feet like a donkey and pretending to wash windows-that-weren't-even-there with her hands. I was a bit

surprised at first but when I did it too,

it was actually lots of fun.

'Keep smiling, girls,' shouted the man.

Laurence Hubert (who is *not* actually

a girl) kept dancing in all the wrong places

This is how to 'wash windows' with your hands

and didn't smile at all. After we'd tapped and shuffled until we were pink, the man with the tummy said: 'Excellent! Well done, my little cherubs. It's time to take a break.'

We had squash and biscuits while Miss Shuffle and the man with the tummy hid behind the piano. Then, after three custard creams and a Jammy Dodger, the man and Miss Shuffle came out:

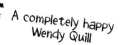

A completely happy Wendy Quill

ACT 2

'We have come to a decision,' said the man

and his tummy. 'The final six dancers for the

SUMMER SEASON!

are:

Ella Pufflestone,
Imogen Brown,
Sara-Jane Clump,
Florence Hubert,
Henrietta Whistleton',
and Wendy . . . '

'How does he know my name?' I gasped.

'Because it's written on your T-shirt, Dumbo,' giggled Florence Hubert. (She doesn't usually call me Dumbo unless it's a special occasion.)

FACT: Without my 'Wendy' T-shirt, no one would have known who I was

'Wendy, erm, well.' The man with the tummy tried to find me on his list. But I wasn't there so he looked at me again: 'Wendy . . . *is a little Princess*,' he said beaming, like it was a very good joke.

'My name is actually Wendy *Quill*,' I said. 'And *not* "a little Princess".' (If people kept getting my name wrong, I'd never be a little bit famous!)

76

'And how do you spell *Quill*?' asked
Miss Shuffle.

'The right way,' I said, politely.

She sniffed into her hand. Then she
scribbled something down and passed
me a letter with my name on it. Florence
Hubert got one too.

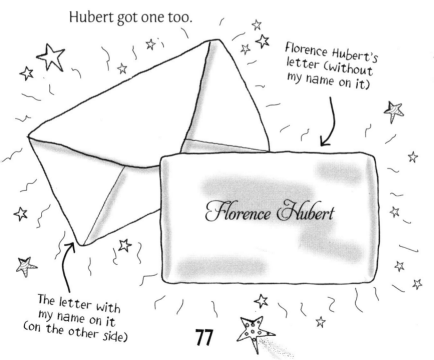

Florence Hubert's letter (without my name on it)

Florence Hubert

The letter with my name on it (on the other side)

77

'Oh!' squealed Florence Hubert.

'We're going to be in

'Are we?' I said, all full of surprise.

'But what about poor Laurence?'

gasped Ms Hubert.

'Maybe next year,' said Miss Shuffle.

'But he's never missed a single

session! And Wendy Quill has only . . .'

Miss Shuffle looked at me so I did my

very ⸱best smile.⸱

'My dear lady,' said the man

with a tummy, 'your son may

have many gifts. But he's

got two left feet and

dances like an elephant.'

Ms Hubert gasped

again and put her hands over

Laurence Hubert's ears.

But Laurence Hubert didn't mind.

'Can I go to football practice now?'

he asked.

Everyone has a
best smile. This
is actually mine

79

No one talked in the car. Florence Hubert was singing quietly. Laurence Hubert was playing on his DS. And Ms Hubert was 'concentrating on the road'. So I got my special notebook out of my bag and looked at my list. I was already up to number 3: *Why do some monkeys have blue bottoms?*

It didn't take me long to work it out. In fact, it's really quite simple. Some monkeys have **BLUE BOTTOMS** because **WHITE BOTTOMS** are difficult to keep clean. It's just like socks, really. (I'm not allowed white socks because I wear them in the garden and then they have to go straight in the bin. And my garden's not as dirty as a jungle because it's mainly patio.) I could

feel my face smiling all over. I **LOVE** it

when I work things out all on my own!

When I got home, I gave Mum the

envelope from Miss Shuffle. This is what

it said:

Wendy Quill has been chosen to play a tap-dancing Munchkin in the summer musical *The Wizard of Oz*. Performances begin at 8 p.m. on Thursday, Friday and Saturday nights. Please bring her to the first rehearsal next Tuesday at 7 p.m.

Munchkin costumes will be provided.

I am going to keep this letter FOR EVER!

'A tap-dancing Munchkin?!' said Mum. 'But you can't even tap-dance.'

'Oh yes I can.' I smiled, and did a 'shuffle-toe-hop'.

'But you haven't got any tap shoes,' said Mum. 'And money doesn't grow on trees, you know.'

Tadaaaaa! This is me shuffle-toe-hopping

'Yes I have,' I said, pointing at my

AMAZING SENSIBLE

T-bar

Extra support

SHOES

You know, the ones with ⛨T-BARS⛨ and ⛨EXTRA SUPPORT.⛨

Old things can actually be best!

'Well, blow me down,' laughed Mum. 'I suppose they do look a little bit similar.'

Suddenly, I felt full up of worry. 'Mum,' I said. 'Is a Munchkin like a pumpkin because I don't want to be a vegetable. NOT IN FRONT OF EVERYONE.'

'No,' smiled Mum. 'Munchkins live in Munchkin land. They're little people—and in the book—they always wear blue.'

'That's a good idea,' I said. 'They must be very easy to keep clean.'

Mum blinked.

'Do they say any words?' I asked.

'Oh yes,' said Mum. 'Lots. And they don't just say them. They sing them. Like:

"*The wicked witch is dead*"

and

"*We're off to see the wizard*".

She started to skip around the kitchen.

I couldn't actually believe it. I was going to sing *and* tap-dance *and* wear blue *all at the same time*.

This was so much better than being a

CROCODILE'S BOTTOM!

Florence Hubert practising in her big hoopy skirt!

Me and Florence Hubert practising together

Florence Hubert's skirt practising on its own

tap tap tap tap tap tap tap tap tap tap tap tap tap tap tap tap

Our actual Munchkin costumes were **AMAZING!** Florence Hubert got a blue skirt with a big hoop inside and I got some pedal pushers with buttons on. Then we all got frilly blue shirts and funny white wigs—like the lady who lives across the road (but Mum says it's best not to talk about that. So I won't). Anyway, we did lots of practising in our costumes until we were completely ready. And we *would* have been Munchkins for a

if the **Theatre critic** hadn't come to watch.

Theatre critics are scary people who go to the theatre and tell everybody they've got it all wrong. This one was called Roger Delamere and he wasn't very nice.

Roger Delamere— the really scary theatre critic

'Oh my!' said the man with the tummy (who is actually called Clive). 'I've just seen Roger Delamere in the queue!! A bad review from him and we'll be ruined!' He looked at Florence Hubert and me. 'They don't look like Munchkins, they look like Morris Dancers!' he said.

'What do you want to do?' asked Miss Shuffle.

'Make them look more Munchkin-like,' said Clive.

88

ACT 2

He bit his nails and looked around.
There wasn't much time and the music had
started to play!

Suddenly, I had a GREAT IDEA.
'I know,' I said. 'You could paint the
Munchkins' faces blue. Then we'd look
really clean!'

'Don't be silly, dear,' said the make-up
lady.

Bits of
Clive's
nail that
accidentally
fell into this
book! Yuck!

But Clive said: *'Genius!* No one's
ever thought of that before. Munchkins—
one hundred per cent blue! Quick! Get the
face paints—before the curtain goes up.'

The make-up lady painted our faces
and Clive and his tummy looked pleased.

The make-up lady making us completely blue

And it *would* have been a GREAT IDEA

if something hadn't gone wrong.

'I feel a bit funny,' said Florence Hubert.

'You've probably got "stage fright",'
I said. 'Tawny says that even famous actors
get stage fright and some are actually
sick!'

My sister Tawny knows EVERYTHING!

'Oh,' Florence Hubert said. 'I do feel a

little bit sick.'

I nodded wisely. I **LOVE** having

a big sister who knows all about

the world.

'Does stage fright make

you itch?' asked Florence.

'I think so,' I said. But I

wasn't actually sure about that bit.

'Munchkins, you're on!' beamed

Clive.

We trotted onto the stage, washing windows

with our hands. I banged my feet as hard as

I could so that I was like a real professional.

Me and Florence Hubert being PROFESSIONAL Munchkins

tap tap tap tap
tap tap tap tap
tap tap tap

Then we finished our first dance and stopped.

'Can you see my mum?' asked Florence Hubert.

It was completely dark apart from the light in our eyes.

'No,' I said. 'And I don't think they can see us. They're making them sit in the dark.'

Our hands, waving in all directions

'Let's just wave anyway,' said Florence Hubert.

So we waved in all directions.

'*Stop waving*,' hissed Dorothy.

(Dorothy is the main character and would be allowed in the 'girly gang' because she wears red pointy shoes with heels on.)

94

ACT 2

'You're not supposed to say that!'
I said. 'They're not your words.'

The Wicked Witch was lying under a house, but her stripy leg kicked me HARD.

'Ouch! Stop kicking me,' I said. 'You're supposed to be completely dead!'

The grumpy witch and both of her legs

'She's not very professional, is she?'
tutted Florence Hubert.

'*Shhhhh!*' hissed the dead witch.

The audience started laughing—
even though they weren't supposed to.
(It's not very nice to laugh at a witch,
especially when she's a dead one.)

Then we tap-danced off the creaky
boards and went backstage.

'Florence Hubert,' I said
curiously, 'is all of your face
all right?'

Florence Hubert sort of
mumbled something. But she
didn't look like a blue Munchkin

This is me BEFORE I knew
about the HUGE PROBLEM

any more. She looked like a spiky
fish that puffs up in the sea.

'Oh Lawks!' gasped Clive
and his tummy. 'What the nora did
you put on her face?'

'Just this blue face-paint,' said the
make-up lady, waving a pot.

'It better be "suitable for children".
If not, "Health and Safety" will be on us like
a tonne of bricks!' said Clive.

'Oh dear!' said the make-up lady.

'Don't worry. I think it's actually stage
fright,' I said.

Florence
Hubert
looking like
a spiky
pufferfish

A spiky
pufferfish
looking like
Florence
Hubert

97

Ms Hubert, Laurence Hubert, Mum, Dad, Grandad, Tawny, and Woody all came running backstage.

'What have you done to my daughter?!' cried Ms Hubert.

'It's the "*child-friendly*" face-paint,' said the make-up lady, waving a pot in the air.

'We'd better wash it off then!' said Mum—sorting everything out.

BLUE FACE-PAINT (child-friendly)

Here's the HUGE PROBLEM in a pot

They ran into the toilets and washed off all the blue. And Mum was actually right. Some people *are* **ALLERGIC** to child-friendly blue face-paint and Florence Hubert is one of them. But nobody knew so it was a complete surprise.

'Oh, your poor face,' cried Ms Hubert.

'It looks worse than it is,' said Dad. 'I'll get some antihistamine tablets from the car.'

'Oh, thank you, Mr Quill,' sighed Ms Hubert.

'Who's Aunty Histameen?' asked Woody.

'This is no time for jokes,' said Mum.

Aunty Histameen's special tablets

99

'ANYONE
FOR A
MINTOE?'

shouted Grandad, getting out his bag of mints.

'TURN
YOUR
HEARING AID
ON,'

shouted Mum.

Grandad
always
shares his
mintoes
when tricky
things are
happening

'I CAN'T
HEAR YOU, PET.
MY
HEARING AID'S
SWITCHED OFF,'

shouted Grandad.

100

'*Will you all please be quiet*!' hissed Clive.

'There's a **Critic** in the audience,'

I explained. 'And he might completely ruin

us all!'

'What's he going to do?' asked Woody.

'I don't know. But it's really bad.'

'Piffle and nonsense,' said Mum.

Grandad passed Florence Hubert a

mintoe. But when she put it in her mouth,

she couldn't suck or anything!

'You can't even eat sweets!' I said,

realizing how terrible it was.

Luckily, Dad gave Florence Hubert one

of his Aunty Histameen's tablets (that was

actually 'safe for children') and suddenly,

Florence Hubert stopped being a fish and
turned into my best friend again!

'Are you all better?' I asked, giving her

another Mintoe.

'Yes, thank you,' she sucked, normally.

Florence Hubert
sucking a sweet
normally. Phew!

'It's nearly time for

THE GRAND FINALE,'

I said.

'Oh,' she said, quietly, ' . . . I don't really think I *want* to be a tap-dancing blue Munchkin any more.'

'Don't you?' I said.

'No. Are you cross?'

'Of course not!' I said. 'Actually,

I don't want to be a tap-dancing blue

Munchkin any more either.'

I am NEVER going to be a tap-dancing blue Munchkin EVER AGAIN!

'Really!?' said Florence Hubert, full of

surprise.

'No,' I said. 'Not if it makes you

ALLERGIC.'

Florence Hubert grinned. 'I don't

mind if you still want to be . . .'

104

'I *don't* still want to be,' I said. 'And anyway, I can be a little bit famous another time.'

'Good old *Wheezy Bird.*' Dad winked.

'I

TOLD YOU.
SHE'S ALL RIGHT
THAT ONE,'

shouted Grandad, fiddling with his

hearing aid.

Mum told Clive that we didn't want to be tap-dancing Munchkins any more. But he didn't actually mind. He said that

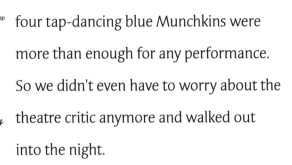

four tap-dancing blue Munchkins were
more than enough for any performance.
So we didn't even have to worry about the
theatre critic anymore and walked out
into the night.

'See you at school,' said Florence
Hubert, waving goodbye.

'Yeah,' I grinned, happily. I was glad
that Florence Hubert wasn't a **FISH** any
more. 'See you at school,' I shouted back.

Tawny, Woody, Grandad and Dad
were already sitting in the car. So it was
actually just me and Mum.

'You've made me proud tonight,' said
Mum. 'It's not easy giving up a part in

The perfect
number of
Munchkins

106

THE WIZARD OF OZ

Even if it is for your best friend.'

'But Mum,' I said, 'you *shouldn't* be proud because it was actually *all my fault*! The blue face-paint was *my* idea.'

Mum hugged me. 'And it was a BRILLIANT idea. How could *you* have known that Florence Hubert was **ALLERGIC** to face-paint?'

My mum's 'proud' hugs are actually the best

'I didn't know,' I said, in a blue kind of way.

'Exactly,' said Mum, squeezing me even tighter. 'There. I'm still proud.'

'Thanks, Mum. ' I grinned. Then I sighed. I couldn't help being a *little* bit sad. It was tricky not being famous for

ACT 2

A WHOLE SUMMER SEASON

any more.

'I know what'll make you feel better,'
said Mum. 'I think you deserve a little treat.
Why don't I buy you a beautiful pair of
slip-on shoes for next term? Then you can
be part of the "girly gang".'

'No, thank you,' I said.

'Don't you want to be part of the "girly gang"?' asked Mum.

'Not really,' I said. 'I don't want to walk like a bow-legged chicken, even if it's not a SCIENTIFIC FACT.'

Mum laughed. 'Well, there must be *something* you fancy?'

'Well,' I smiled, 'there *is* actually something I'd really, really like . . . '

'Go on . . . ' said Mum. 'What is it?'

'Well, what I'd really, really like is . . .

A BRAND NEW PAIR of AMAZING SENSIBLE SHOES—with T-BARS and EXTRA SUPPORT!'

Woody Quill: my big brother all bursting with amazing ideas

Tyler Ainsworth: looks like he's done something wrong again

Me—Wendy Quill: being slightly full up of plague

Kevin: the 'not-very-Spanish' school rat

Angelina Hardthorpe: screaming with both of her arms

ACT 3
WENDY QUILL CATCHES THE PLAGUE

'Hi, it's me again!'

Everybody has a 'pet hate': something
they *completely* don't like. Tawny
hates it when *my* things go on *her*
side of the room and throws them back
straight away. Woody hates it when old
ladies stroke his hair and say: 'I'd pay for
curls like that!' And Dad hates it when you
don't 'put the plug in and have a proper

wash'. But Mum's 'pet hate' is much

worse because Mum's pet hate is actually

all my fault. Mum hates it when I forget

IMPORTANT LETTERS at the

bottom of my school bag.

A slightly
squashed
VERY
IMPORTANT
letter

I don't *try* and forget about

IMPORTANT LETTERS. I'm just

that sort of person—the forgetting-things

sort. This term, I've forgotten to 'dress up in magenta', 'check thoroughly for nits', and 'bring something soft to "show and tell"'. Anyway, I was having a completely normal night trying to go to sleep when Mum ran in and switched on the light!

'*Wendy Dotterel Quill*!' she said (which is what she calls me when she's cross). 'Why on earth didn't you tell me that you had an IMPORTANT LETTER at the bottom of your school bag?'

It's tricky to remember what NOT to forget

'Sorry, I forgot,' I said, because I actually had. 'Is it a VERY IMPORTANT LETTER?'

117

She read it out loud:

Oh Wednesday, please make sure your child wears sombre colours. Miss Pinch's class will be doing The Plague.

I don't really like 'sombre' colours

'Oh no!' I gasped, all full up of shock.

'Is Wednesday tomorrow or today?'

'Tomorrow of course!' said Mum.

118

'Oh no!' I groaned again.

'Exactly,' said Mum. Her face looked all pointy and not like her usual one at all. So I tried to change the subject.

'What does "sombre" actually mean, Mum?' I asked curiously.

'Miserable,' said Mum, picking up my socks. 'You know, browns, blacks, and greys.'

'But I haven't got any "miserable" clothes!' I said. 'I've only got flowers and stripes. And Woody only wears football shirts. And Tawny only wears blue! What am I going to do?'

Mum—with her 'pointy face' on

119

Dad's . . . jumper

Dad's . . . jumper

Dad's . . . jumper

'Calm down,' said Mum. 'Your dad does a good line in "sombre".'

Mum was actually right. Dad's got lots of 'sombre' clothes because he's a birdwatcher and has to be camouflaged. But my tummy felt like it was going to fall out.

'Mum,' I said, 'I *can't* wear Dad's clothes because the 'girly gang' will laugh at me and no one will sit by me at lunch!'

'Well, that's no bad thing if you've got **THE PLAGUE**,' said Mum.

Dad's
favourite black
bird-watching
jumper

'I'm not actually joking,' I said. 'I *can't* wear Dad's clothes.'

'Sorry, love,' said Mum. 'But you should have thought about that yesterday.'

PET HATE ALERT:
I THINK THIS IS ACTUALLY MY PET HATE:
'YOU SHOULD HAVE THOUGHT ABOUT THAT YESTERDAY.'

It's completely silly to tell someone they should have thought about something yesterday. Because they haven't. And they didn't. And it's too late now!

In the morning, the alarm clock broke

so we didn't have time for any breakfast.

Woody said that was a good thing because

it would make me look poorly and sick.

'But I don't look like I've got **THE**

PLAGUE though,' I said, peering into

the mirror.

I wasn't looking nearly-dead at all!

'Don't move,' he said, getting some plasters out of the medicine bag.

'What are you doing?' I asked, even though I knew because he was sticking plasters all over my face.

'Just wait.' He grinned mysteriously.

When he'd used up all the plasters, he took a purple felt tip out of his pocket. (He always keeps felt tips in his pockets in case of emergencies.) Then he drew lots of big purple spots on top of the plasters.

'That is AMAZING!' I gasped. 'I look completely full up of **PLAGUE** now!'

Sometimes, Woody is almost like a GENIUS!

123

Woody . . . covering
me up with PLASTERS
and PLAGUE

'Wendy Dotterel Quill! You're not even dressed!' yelled Mum.

I ran upstairs and put on Dad's most miserabilitive bird-watching jumper. (Sometimes you have to make up words like 'miserabilitive' because they're not actually already there.) Then I grabbed a pair of leggings from Tawny's side of the room and wriggled into them as fast as I could.

'Hurry up or I'll leave without you,' shouted Mum. (This is another silly thing that grown-ups say. Mum wouldn't really leave

Me—doing my best 'sombre' face

without us because she'd just have to come back again. Or get a baby sitter. Or get in trouble with the police. And then we'd be even *more* late.)

I ran down the stairs and had another quick look in the mirror.

'Pull a nearly dead face,' said Woody.

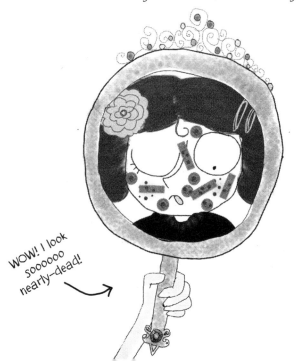

WOW! I look soooooo nearly-dead!

I did and it was BRILLIANT!

'Well I must say,' said Mum. 'You do look rather convincing.'

'Thank you,' I whispered in my poorliest voice. 'I'll practise my cough in the car.'

SOME INTERESTING FACTS
ABOUT THE PLAGUE
(THAT ARE ACTUALLY REALLY TRUE):

FACT 1

The Plague was spread by lots of rats that came on ships from Spain.

Sophia Nowitsky—interrupting again

'But Miss Pinch,' interrupted Sophia Nowitsky. 'In my encyclopaedia, it says that *fleas* spread the **PLAGUE**, *not* rats.'

'Well,' said Miss Pinch, 'technically, your encyclopaedia may be correct. But the fleas needed something to live on. And they lived on Spanish rats.

I don't exactly know why I made my Spanish rats pirates

And today we'll be making wonderful rats out of these newspaper and tights.' She waved some old socks in the air. 'But first, we must learn some more facts!' I wrote down some more facts as fast as I could:

SOME MORE INTERESTING FACTS ABOUT THE PLAGUE:

FACT 2

Everybody started dying and getting purple lumps under their armpits.

(Diagram: these are actually called 'buboes' and do not look very nice.)

FACT 3

The King killed all the cats and dogs because he got it wrong. Then there were even more rats (because the cats and dogs weren't eating them). So it was a really big shame.

FACT 4

People starting whipping their backs because they thought The Plague was a punishment from God. But that did not make them feel better. Actually, it made them feel worse because now they had The Plague and hurting backs.

FACT 5

A man with a cart shouted: 'Bring out your dead' a lot.

FACT 6

Some people wore dead frogs around their necks and some doctors wore white beaks. But that didn't stop them catching it.

Cough! Cough! Cough! Cough! Cough! Cough! Cough! Cough!

That's not very nice!

Then we made rats out of newspaper,

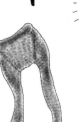

socks and tights and they looked

TOTALLY BRILLIANT.

'We should do **THE PLAGUE** more

often.' Miss Pinch smiled.

'Miss Pinch,' I said. 'Where is Tyler

Ainsworth?'

We all looked round. But suddenly,

Tyler Ainsworth was all gone!

'Oh heavens!' gasped Miss Pinch. But

the bell was ringing and it was playtime.

Playtime with **THE PLAGUE** is really

good fun. We tried to do hopscotch but

kept falling on top of each other. Then we

I LOVE making rats out of socks

coughed a bit. And then we leant against

the netball courts and GROANED.

'Be quiet,' said Mrs Rudgerford, coming

over to us. 'The A team are having their

photos taken for the local *Gazette*. We don't

want to put them off now, do we?'

'No we don't,' I groaned politely.

And I LOVE
having THE
PLAGUE
with Florence
Hubert

133

'Watch your tongue, Wendy Quill,' said Mrs Rudgerford—even though I still had **THE PLAGUE**.

The 'A team' were holding a golden trophy and looked all shiny and tall.

'What happened to your face?' asked the photographer (when he'd finished doing his job).

'I've got **THE PLAGUE**,' I said. 'And I'm covered in bubonic purple spots.'

'They look like plasters to me,' said the photographer.

The 'A team' with some of their hands

'Well, they're not,' said Florence

Hubert. '**THE PLAGUE** is very outrageous

and if we sneeze on you, you'll die.'

'Well,' sighed the photographer.

'At least the Black Death is quick . . .'

A QUICK IMPORTANT FACT:

THE BLACK DEATH is another way of saying THE PLAGUE—but with a lot less Ps and Gs. And Tawny says it was CONTAGIOUS not OUTRAGEOUS—but I'm not sure if that's true.

' . . . Mine's a slow death, mine is,'

carried on the photographer. 'Taking pictures

of netball teams and prize-winning vegetables *every single day*.' The fed-up photographer looked *really* sad.

'But *some* vegetables can be very exciting,' I said, trying to cheer him up. 'My Grandad grew a carrot that looked like a fat lady on a swing.'

'Did he?' asked Florence Hubert.

I nodded a great big 'YES'.

'When I was your age,' said the fed-up photographer, 'I thought I'd travel the world . . . I was going to be a foreign correspondent.'

'Well, you do look a bit foreign,' I said. 'Your nose is really nice and big.'

Grandad's
AMAZING
lady carrot

TOP SECRET: Florence Hubert said the photographer was 'a little bit gorgeous'

'Yeah,' smiled Florence Hubert. 'And so is your coat.'

He mumbled something under his breath. Then he picked up his bag and walked off!

I was so busy having **THE PLAGUE** at playtime that I'd almost forgotten about wanting to be a little bit famous. And if it hadn't been for Tyler Ainsworth, I probably wouldn't be at all. You see, when we got back inside, Tyler Ainsworth was already sitting at his desk.

'Well,' said Miss Pinch. 'This *is* a first! I'm so glad we've found a topic that you find of interest, Tyler Ainsworth.'

ACT 3

Tyler Ainsworth grinned.

'Now,' began Miss Pinch. 'Today, we've been learning about how the rats spread **THE PLAGUE** across Europe, and we've made a wonderful collection of our own rats out of newspaper and socks.' She looked at the display table and we all sighed happily.

Awwwww! I never knew sock-rats could look sooooo professional

But suddenly, Miss Pinch

S-C-R-E-A-M-E-D-!

'AAAA

RRRHH

HHHHH

ARRRRR
HHHHHH
HHHHH!'

· And *then* she jumped

onto a box and pointed at her bag.

Tyler Ainsworth grinned a bit more.

'There's a . . . RAT in my
handbag!' cried Miss Pinch.

141

The page before . . . Miss Pinch is actually very good at screaming

A long tail wiggled in the air. I knew who it was straight away.

'It's not just *any* rat, Miss Pinch' I said. 'I think it's actually Kevin.'

Kevin is our school rat. I know him really well because he came to live with us in the holidays.

This is Kevin— not being Spanish at all!

'I don't care if he's the King of England!' cried Miss Pinch. 'Get him out of my bag!!!'

I tried to pick him up but he jumped

onto the floor and ran towards Angelina

Hardthorpe.

'AARRHHHH!'

screamed the 'girly gang' all at once.

Fact: The girly gang do not like rats

Kevin was frightened and leapt up onto Angelina Hardthorpe's desk but she actually

fainted because she's not used to that sort of thing.

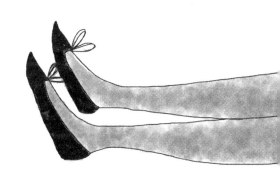

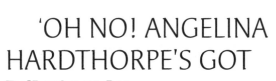

'OH NO! ANGELINA HARDTHORPE'S GOT THE PLAGUE!' shouted Tyler Ainsworth, which was completely *not* true.

'Has she?' asked Florence Hubert, getting all confused. 'Gosh! Maybe Kevin's got Spanish fleas!'

'Of course he hasn't got Spanish fleas,' I said. 'Kevin's an *English* rat and he's only been on holiday in my house. And anyway, *no one* gets THE PLAGUE any more.'

But everybody was too busy being scared.

Suddenly, Kevin remembered me and ran towards my legs.

'AARRHHH!'

screamed Sophia Nowitsky.

'STOP HIM!'

cried Miss Pinch.

I had just scooped Kevin up (just like a PROPER vet) when someone suddenly opened the door. There was a **BIG** . . .

I wish I had a rat all of my own . . .

It was the fed-up photographer. But
he wasn't fed-up any more.

'Thank you,' he laughed. 'You've made
my day.'

This might seem like a sad story because
Angelina Hardthorpe fainted and
Tyler Ainsworth had to go and see the
headmaster. But actually, it isn't. You see,
the day after Kevin escaped and I'd caught

THE PLAGUE, Grandad came round for
tea. His cheeks were all pink and excitable:

'Well, Ducky,' he said, throwing his
favourite newspaper across the table,
'I always knew you'd make the headlines.'

Only
Grandad
is allowed
to drink
out of his
special cup

I looked at the paper. I completely couldn't believe it! There I was! Right on the front page—where EVERYONE COULD SEE!!!

PRIMARY SCHOOL PLAGUE FIASCO

Disaster struck at a local primary school when Kevin, the school rat, was released into a screaming Plague Workshop!

Mayhem ensued as children fainted and staff took refuge on their desks! But fortunately for runaway rodent Kevin, Wendy Quill (age 9— pictured with purple bubonic spots) rescued pesky pet and put an end to Plague Panic!

Hooray! I am a little bit FAMOUS!

'Oh look! I'm rescuing Kevin!' I said, because I actually was.

'Wow!' said Woody. 'That is *so* cool.'

'Not bad, little sis.' Tawny smiled.

I blushed and didn't say anything because nobody likes a show off.

Mum put the picture of me rescuing Kevin in a special frame on my wall. Florence Hubert says it looks **AMAZING** and **REALLY PROFESSIONAL**. And it does. But sometimes, when I look at it before I go to sleep, I wish I was wearing something a bit more nice. Like my favourite daisy T-shirt or my stripy hat.

Kevin and me in our 'really special frame'

153

Not Dad's ENORMOUS bird-watching jumper and lots of plasters and purple spots.

But *then* I remember that if I *hadn't* caught **THE PLAGUE** and rescued Kevin, then I wouldn't be on the FRONT PAGE of the newspaper. And if I *hadn't been* on the FRONT PAGE of the newspaper, then I *wouldn't* be a little bit famous. And if I *wasn't* a little bit famous, then everybody would forget my real name—which *isn't* really *Wheezy Bird.* It is actually

WENDY QUILL.

Dad's sombre black bird-watching jumper and my bright purple bubonic plasters

154

The (Completely Happy) End

very spotty

EXTRA BITS THAT ARE A TOTAL SURPRISE

BiT ONE:

WENDY QUILL'S
INCOMPLETE LIST OF THINGS
TO THINK ABOUT WHEN SITTING
ON THE SIDE . . .

Here's a list I actually started earlier—but if you like, you can get a piece of paper and finish it all by yourself. Then you'll be completely ready when you need to sit on the side . . .

- ♥ Why have people got two legs and not six or four?

- ♥ Where do ice-cream vans go in winter?

- ♥ Why don't vegetables make your teeth rot?

- ♥ Do newsreaders ever pick their nose?

- ♥ Why are trees green (and not pink or something else)?

- ♥ How do people know that elephants never forget?

- ♥ When dogs cry, do they actually mean it?

- ♥ Can a spider eat too many flies?

♥ Who puts the bubbles in lemonade?

♥ Why don't grown-ups do handstands?

♥ Who invented the whole Time thing?

♥ Why do cats have 'flaps' and not 'doors'?

♥ Do all big sisters know EVERYTHING already?

If you have lots more **THINGS TO THINK ABOUT WHEN SITTING ON THE SIDE**, please send me them in case I run out. You might even win a '**THINGS TO THINK ABOUT WHEN SITTING ON THE SIDE**' Notebook!

Email: wendywheezybirdquill@gmail.com

BiT TWO:

WENDY QUiLL'S
TOP TiPS ON HOW TO GET
A LiTTLE BiT FAMOUS

Wendy is a Little Princess

Tip 1:

Try to wear a T-shirt with your name on it.

Then no one will forget who you are. (If you

can't find one, don't worry, you can actually

make your own with a pen.)

Um, check with an adult first before you get that pen!

Tip 2:

Make sure people have their hearing aids switched on. Otherwise, they won't always hear you.

Tip 3:

If someone important takes your photograph, make sure you do your very best smile. (The one where you show all of your teeth at the same time.)

A really useful camera is handy

Learn to smile with all of your teeth

164

EXTRA BITS THAT ARE A TOTAL SURPRISE

Remember: being a crocodile's bottom can actually be fun

Tip 4:

Don't be sad if you don't get *picked*.

Sometimes it's better to be a **CROCODILE'S BOTTOM**. Or even a dog.

Tip 5:

If you laugh like a sea-lion people might forget your name, so learn how to do **SPECIAL TRICK 1** *(see page 63)*. (I don't know why but people who laugh like sea-lions don't normally get a little bit famous. Not in this country, anyway.)

Ha Ha
Ha Ha
Ha Ha

I think I have a very nice laugh!

Tip 6:

This is the most important one and that's why I saved it till last:

NEVER, EVER try to be like everybody else because then you'll be just the same!

GOOD LUCK!

166

ABOUT THE AUTHOR AND THE ILLUSTRATOR

WENDY MEDDOUR was a crocodile's bottom (instead of a 'Wendy') in her very first school play. She also (completely accidentally) auditioned to be a bubble-gum blowing tap-dancer and spent a whole summer season shuffle-toe-hopping in her amazing-sensible-shoes! But the 'run-away-rat in the classroom' chapter is completely made up. In real life, it was a snake.

HISTORICAL EVIDENCE:
This is an actual, real photograph of Wendy Meddour being a crocodile's bottom

When no one was looking, Mina May added Miss Pinch, Henna Hussein and Wendy Quill to the 'evidence'

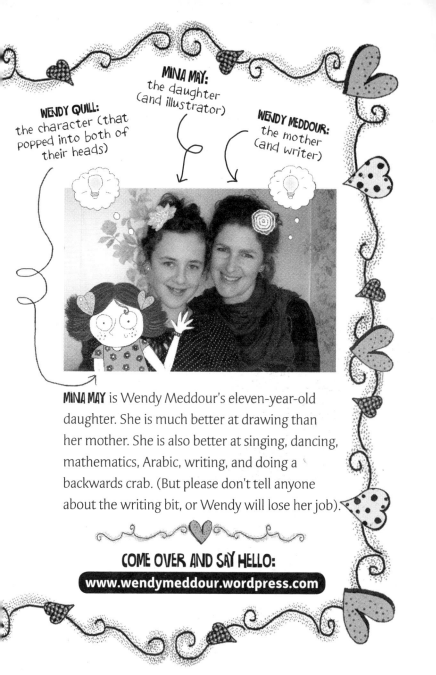

WENDY QUILL: the character (that popped into both of their heads)

MINA MAY: the daughter (and illustrator)

WENDY MEDDOUR: the mother (and writer)

MINA MAY is Wendy Meddour's eleven-year-old daughter. She is much better at drawing than her mother. She is also better at singing, dancing, mathematics, Arabic, writing, and doing a backwards crab. (But please don't tell anyone about the writing bit, or Wendy will lose her job).

COME OVER AND SAY HELLO:

www.wendymeddour.wordpress.com

LOOK OUT FOR THE NEXT HILARIOUS CAPER: